Little Rabbit's New Baby

written and illustrated by

HARRY HORSE

PEACHTREE
ATLANTA

For my sister Kay

Published by
PEACHTREE PUBLISHERS
1700 Chattahoochee Avenue
Atlanta, Georgia 30318-2112
www.peachtree-online.com

Text and Illustrations © 2006 by Harry Horse

Illustrations created in pen and ink and watercolor

First published in Great Britain in 2006 by Penguin Books
First United States edition published in 2008 by Peachtree Publishers

Printed in China
10 9 8 7 6 5 4 3 2 1
First Edition

Library of Congress Cataloging-in-Publication Data

Horse, Harry.
  Little Rabbit's new baby / written and illustrated by Harry Horse.-- 1st ed.
      p. cm.
  Summary: Little Rabbit has looked forward to becoming a big brother, but when Mama brings home triplets, he quickly realizes that babies are not as much fun as he thought they would be.
  ISBN-13: 978-1-56145-431-0 / ISBN-10: 1-56145-431-1
  [1. Babies--Fiction. 2. Triplets--Fiction. 3. Brothers and sisters--Fiction. 4. Rabbits--Fiction.] I. Title.
  PZ7.H7885Lmn 2007
  [E]--dc22
                              2007034158

Little Rabbit was very excited. Mama was going to have a baby. "Hurry up, baby," said Little Rabbit. "Come out of my mama's tummy and play with me."

Little Rabbit couldn't wait to show the baby how to play fun games.
He would teach the baby how to hop and how to skip.

"Babies like hopping and skipping," he told Grandma.
Grandma said that he would be the best brother a baby
could have. Little Rabbit was very proud.

Mama went to the hospital to have the baby and Papa took Little Rabbit to visit. Little Rabbit hopped and skipped all the way there.

The rabbit hospital was very big. There were lots of baby rabbits there.
But there was only one baby that Little Rabbit wanted to see.

"Mama!" cried Little Rabbit. "Where's my new baby?"

But there wasn't one baby. There were three babies! Papa had to sit down. The nurse gave him a cup of tea. Three babies!

Papa took Mama and the triplets home. Little Rabbit pushed the baby carriage. He would not let anyone help him, even when it was hard to push.

Little Rabbit showed everybody the new babies. "I am their big brother," he said.

When they got home, Mama let Little Rabbit hold the new babies.

Little Rabbit hugged them
and kissed them.

He blew softly down their ears to
tickle them.

The new babies started to cry.

Little Rabbit wanted the babies to sleep in his bed with him. But Mama decided they would be more comfortable in the cradle. Papa agreed. "These babies are still very small," he said. "They need all the rest they can get."

Little Rabbit wanted the babies to play with Charlie Horse.
"No, Little Rabbit," said Papa. "They are only little babies. They
don't want to play with Charlie Horse yet. Let them rest a while."

The next morning, Little Rabbit woke up very early. He wanted to play with the babies, but they were still asleep. Then Little Rabbit had an idea. He would make them some breakfast.

Mama would be pleased.

Little Rabbit got the babies out of bed. What would they like to eat?

He tried carrots, because all rabbits like carrots.
But not the babies. They threw the carrots on the floor.

"Oh, Little Rabbit!" cried Mama. "What a mess!"

"It's the babies' fault," said Little Rabbit. "They don't know how to eat."

Mama carried the babies back to bed.

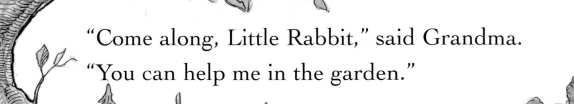

"Come along, Little Rabbit," said Grandma.
"You can help me in the garden."

But Little Rabbit could not think about anything but the new babies. When Grandma went to sleep in her chair, Little Rabbit crept back inside the house.

"Not asleep again!" said Little Rabbit.
"Come along, you sleepy heads. Wake up!"

He got the babies out of bed. "I am Little Rabbit, your big brother.
I will show you how to play some really fun games."

But the babies were not as good at games as Little Rabbit thought they would be. They didn't know how to play with the rocket.

They didn't know how to catch the ball.

And they nearly broke Charlie Horse.

Little Rabbit scolded them. The babies started to cry.

Mama was upset. Not with the babies—with Little Rabbit.
"It's not fair," said Little Rabbit. "Those babies are all that
Mama thinks about now."

But the babies seemed to like Little Rabbit. They followed him around all over the place. Wherever he went, there were the babies. "Go away," shouted Little Rabbit. "Why don't you leave me alone?"

When he tried to play with his balloon, there they were again. They wanted to touch Charlie Horse. They wanted to play with his rocket. Their sticky paws got everywhere.

"Leave my things alone!" cried Little Rabbit.

When he wanted to watch *The Moon Rabbits,* they were there too, crawling all over his things. "Go away!" cried Little Rabbit. Papa told him not to shout at the babies.

"Mama and Papa don't want me any more!" he sobbed. "All they think about are those babies."

Little Rabbit hid under the bed. Then he heard the babies crying. He put his paws over his ears.

Grandma tried to get the babies
to go to sleep, but they cried
even more.

Mama and Papa tried to get the
babies to sleep, but they cried
even louder.

Poor Mama and Papa. They looked so tired.

Little Rabbit had an idea.

He brought the rocket, Charlie Horse, and his red balloon to show the babies. As soon as the babies saw Little Rabbit they stopped crying. He let them play with the rocket.

He let them play with Charlie Horse (even though their paws were sticky).

He let them play with his red balloon.

And when the babies grew sleepy, he rocked their cradle until they fell fast asleep.

"Good night and sleep tight," whispered Little Rabbit.

Mama was so pleased. She hugged Little Rabbit and kissed him. "Thank you Little Rabbit. You are the best help a mama could have."

And after that, everywhere those little rabbits went,

Little Rabbit went too.